RAINBOW
magic ®

The Magical Animal Fairies

For Isabelle Hudson,
with lots of love and
fairy sparkles

Special thanks to
Sue Mongredien

ORCHARD BOOKS

First published in Great Britain in 2009 by Orchard Books
This edition published in 2016 by The Watts Publishing Group

7 9 10 8 6

Copyright © 2009 Rainbow Magic Limited.
Copyright © 2009 HIT Entertainment Limited.
Illustrations copyright © Orchard Books, 2009

HIT entertainment

A CIP catalogue record for this book is available from the British Library.

ISBN 978 1 40830 349 8

Printed in Great Britain by Clays Ltd, St Ives plc

MIX
Paper from
responsible sources
FSC   FSC® C104740
www.fsc.org

The paper and board used in this book are made from wood from responsible sources

Orchard Books
An imprint of Hachette Children's Group
Part of The Watts Publishing Group Limited
Carmelite House, 50 Victoria Embankment, London EC4Y 0DZ

An Hachette UK Company
www.hachette.co.uk
www.hachettechildrens.co.uk

Ashley the Dragon Fairy

by Daisy Meadows

ORCHARD

There are seven special animals,
Who live in Fairyland.
They use their magic powers
To help others where they can.

A dragon, black cat, firebird,
A seahorse and snow swan too,
A unicorn and ice bear -
I know just what to do.

I'll lock them in my castle
And never let them out.
The world will turn more miserable,
Of that, I have no doubt...

Contents

Contents

The Adventure Begins!

"Bye, Mum, bye, Dad!" Kirsty Tate yelled, waving as her parents' car pulled away.

Her mum, who was in the passenger seat, rolled down the window. "See you next week," she called. "And have a wonderful time, both of you!"

Kirsty grinned at her best friend, Rachel Walker. "We will!" both girls chorused.

A whole week away at an outdoor adventure camp – it was going to be just perfect!

"Hi guys," came a voice from behind them. They turned to see a tall, smiling girl with long brown hair, whose red T-shirt had "Adventure Camp Counsellor" printed on in yellow letters. "You must be Kirsty and Rachel," she said. "I'm Lucy, one of the counsellors here. I'll take you to your cabin, OK?"

Kirsty and Rachel followed Lucy along a path, feeling very excited. They passed through a small wooded area where Rachel spotted a squirrel bounding up one of the pine trees, and then out to a sunny meadow with rolling hills beyond it. There were wooden cabins dotted here and there, each with colourful curtains at the window, and brightly painted front doors. Music floated from some of the cabins, and Kirsty and Rachel could see clusters of other campers having fun. There was a basketball ring attached to one of the trees and a group of boys were shooting hoops. A couple of girls were messing about on skateboards outside another cabin, laughing and chatting.

"Here we are," Lucy said just then, veering away to a cabin on the right. It had a light blue door and blue gingham curtains at the windows. "I'll let you unpack, then I suggest you explore the camp to get your bearings. There are maps everywhere, so you won't get lost. We'll all be going on a caving trip in about an hour, OK?"

Kirsty and Rachel thanked Lucy, then entered the cabin feeling curious and excited about their home for the next week.

There was a bunk bed and four single
beds, a separate bathroom and a
couple of posters on the
walls. Rachel hurled
herself onto the lower
bunk and Kirsty
dumped her
cardigan on
the top bunk
to bag it.
  "Wow, look
at this," Kirsty
said, spotting
a timetable.
"Canoeing, horse-
riding, swimming…
There's so much to do here!"
"I can't wait to meet the other
girls in our cabin," Rachel said, smiling.

"And you never know… We might even make some new fairy friends while we're here, too!"

Kirsty beamed at the thought. She and Rachel were good friends with the fairies, and they'd had lots of adventures with them. Magical things just seemed to happen whenever the two of them got together! "Come on, let's explore," she suggested. "We can unpack later. I'm dying to look around!"

Rachel agreed, and the girls left their bags and headed out into the sunshine again.

There was a large building in the
centre of the campsite with a sign above
the double doors that read "Clubhouse".
Near to it was a wooden signpost with
arrows pointing in different directions –
one said "Canteen", another read "Sports
Pitches" and a third said "Outdoor
Amphitheatre".

"Look, there's a map here," Rachel
said, pointing to a colourful sign in
a glass case, just outside the clubhouse.
She and
Kirsty
strolled
over to it.

"Ooh, a waterfall," Kirsty said, showing Rachel on the map.

"And there are the stables," Rachel noticed. She blinked. The sun was shining very brightly onto the glass case, making it sparkle. She shielded her eyes. Suddenly the light seemed dazzling!

Kirsty was blinking and looking away too. "The sun is so strong," she commented. "I wish I had my sunglasses!"

Rachel was about to reply when another voice was heard. "Kirsty! Rachel! This is King Oberon. The fairies need your help. Please use your magic lockets to come to Fairyland as soon as you can!"

Rachel gasped. So the sparkling light from the glass case was fairy magic! She grabbed Kirsty's hand and pulled her around the side of the clubhouse, where nobody could see them.

"Come on," she said, fiddling with the catch of the special locket she always wore around her neck. "Oh, I hope the fairies are all right!"

Kirsty was busy with her own locket. Inside there was some magical fairy dust, given to them by the fairy queen herself. They each took a pinch and sprinkled it over themselves, then held hands as a magical sparkly whirlwind began spinning around them. Another fairy adventure was beginning!

Off to Fairyland!

Moments later, the girls felt themselves being gently set down, and the whirlwind spun away. They blinked and looked around. "The Fairyland Palace!" Kirsty cried in delight, seeing it in front of them.

"And there are Queen Titania and King Oberon," Rachel realised. "Come on!"

The two friends ran over to the fairy king and queen, who were standing with a group of other fairies that the girls didn't recognise. As usual, Rachel and Kirsty had shrunk down to fairy-size now that they were in Fairyland.

"Hello again, Kirsty and Rachel," King Oberon said. He didn't seem his usual cheerful self, Kirsty noticed, and she wondered why. "We've called you here because unfortunately Jack Frost is up to his tricks again. This time he's really gone too far! He's stolen seven Magical Animals from our fairies –

a dragon, a black cat, a firebird, a seahorse, a snow swan, a unicorn and an ice bear."

"Why?" Rachel asked. "What does he want with them?"

Queen Titania joined in the conversation. "These are our Magical Animal Fairies," she said, pointing to the group of seven fairies who stood with her. "And every Spring, they get seven new young Magical Animals to look

after and train for one year. Each
Magical Animal has special qualities and
helps spread the kind of magic that every
human and fairy can possess – the magic
of imagination, luck, humour, friendship,
compassion, healing and courage. The
fairies spend a whole year teaching the
baby animals how to use and control
their powers."

Kirsty felt she still didn't quite
understand and was about to ask a
question when one of the Magical
Animal Fairies stepped forwards. Her
hair was in an afro style and she wore
combat trousers, embroidered with a
dragon on one leg, and a stripy vest
top. "Hi there," she said. "I'm Ashley the
Dragon Fairy, and this is Lara the Black
Cat Fairy, Erin the Firebird Fairy,

Rihanna the Seahorse Fairy, Sophia the Snow Swan Fairy, Leona the Unicorn Fairy and Caitlin the Ice Bear Fairy."

Rachel and Kirsty smiled at the seven friendly faces before them. "Hi," Rachel said, curious to know more about these fairies and their animals.

"Each of the Magical Animals looks after a different magical power," Ashley went on. "The baby dragon is responsible for imagination. The black cat looks after luck, the firebird's magical quality is humour and the seahorse is responsible for friendship. The snow swan inspires compassion, the baby unicorn has the power of healing, and the ice bear looks after the power of courage."

"We spend a whole year teaching the baby animals how to use and control their magical powers," Lara added. "Once the Magical Animals are all trained, they go back to their families in Fairyland, where they will help spread their magical gifts throughout the fairy world and the human world."

"But Jack Frost kidnapped the

Magical Animals because he didn't want them to be fully trained," the queen explained. "And if the animals aren't trained, they can't help spread their lovely magical qualities, like imagination and humour – qualities that everyone needs!"

"Jack Frost would like the world to be as miserable as he is," the King added. "He doesn't want people or fairies to have friendship and luck."

Kirsty and Rachel exchanged horrified glances. They couldn't imagine how awful life would be without friendship! And the idea of a world without any humour or courage was too sad for words.

"We'll help," Kirsty said at once. "We'll go to Jack Frost's castle right away and get the young animals back for you!"

The King smiled. "Thank you, Kirsty," he said. "We knew we could count on you and Rachel. However, something remarkable has happened. Come to the Seeing Pool and we can show you."

The King and Queen led the girls and the Magical Animal Fairies to a large blue pool in the palace gardens.

The Queen touched the surface of the water with her wand and it shimmered with all the colours of the rainbow.

A picture started to form on the water – a picture of Jack Frost surrounded by all of the Magical Animals outside his Ice Castle. Rachel giggled as she saw the little dragon sneeze and blast out some flames, melting a part of the icy wall!

"Oh dear," she said. "I don't think Jack Frost will be pleased about that."

"Look at the ice bear!" Kirsty said, pointing to a different area of the picture. A cute white bear was chasing Jack Frost's goblin servants and making them freeze into icy statues by tapping them with its paws.

The girls watched the scene develop into chaos. The Magical Animals were now happily chasing each other around the castle, completely ignoring Jack Frost's orders. And then, suddenly, a sparkling window opened up in one of the castle walls and the seven young animals slipped through it, one after another.

"Where have they gone?" Rachel asked, puzzled.

"Into the human world, it seems," the Queen told her. "And there's Jack Frost sending his goblins through the same window, to track them down!"

The girls watched the picture as a group of the goblin servants scrambled through the magical window and vanished from sight. The window gradually faded away.

"What happened next?" Kirsty asked.

Ashley shrugged unhappily. "We don't know," she said. "The animals must be hiding somewhere in the human world."

"We've got to find them, before anyone else does," Erin added.

"They're so young, they can't control their magical abilities – and they may be causing strange things to happen in the human world!"

"We'll help you find them," Rachel said at once.

"Thank you," said King Oberon. "But you must be careful. As Erin said, the animals aren't able to work their magic very well yet. This might mean that their magical qualities of imagination, luck, humour, friendship, compassion, healing and courage are more powerful than usual. It might even mean that the qualities work in reverse if the animals are nervous."

"The magical qualities will affect anyone who comes near the animals," the Queen said. "So watch out for anybody acting strangely – it may lead you to one of them."

"I'll come to the human world with you to search for Sizzle, the baby dragon," Ashley said. "He's got a cold at the moment – he must have caught it while he was at Jack Frost's Ice Castle. I'm a bit worried about him."

"You must be careful, and stay out of sight," the Queen reminded her. "No one in the human world can know about Fairyland or anyone who lives here. Good luck!"

With those words, she pointed her wand at Ashley, Kirsty and Rachel.

The three of them just had time to call goodbye before another glittery whirlwind whisked them up and took them spinning through the air...

Into the Labyrinth

With a last flurry of sparkles, the girls found themselves back to their usual size, and in the Adventure Camp once again. Ashley looked about eagerly, her gauzy wings shimmering in the sunshine – but then a look of disappointment crossed her face. "We Magical Animal Fairies can always sense when our creatures are nearby," she said, "but I'm not picking up anything here."

She was about to say something else when they heard voices. Ashley darted onto Kirsty's shoulder and hid behind her hair, not wanting to be seen.

"I guess we'd better go back to our cabin," Rachel said. "It must be time to go on the caving trip."

"Keep a look out for dragons," Kirsty whispered excitedly, as they headed off. Oh, it was so wonderful to be starting a new fairy adventure!

Back at their cabin, they saw that
their room-mates had now arrived and
were all unpacking. "Hi," said a blonde
girl wearing a pink baseball cap. "I'm
Emma, and this is Katie, Natasha
and Catherine."

"I'm Rachel and
this is Kirsty,"
Rachel replied.

"Hi," Kirsty said
to them all. She
could feel Ashley
still tucked under
her hair and hoped
that none of the other
girls would spot the little fairy!

Just then, Lucy popped her
head around the door. "Hi everyone,
it's time to set off on our trip," she said.

"We're going to the Labyrinth – some hidden caves deep in the mountain. It'll be cold in there so make sure you wear warm clothes under your waterproofs and thick socks with your walking boots. Oh, and bring some gloves, too!"

The six girls quickly got ready. While everyone was busy, Ashley nipped out from her hiding place and tucked herself into the front pocket of Rachel's coat.

"Hey, what's that?" Natasha asked just then, and Rachel's heart almost stopped, thinking she must have spotted Ashley.

But Natasha was pointing to Rachel's bed, and she saw with a huge rush of relief that Natasha meant a magazine which had fallen out of her bag.

"Oh…it's a new magazine," Rachel replied thankfully. "You can borrow it later if you like."

"Thanks," Natasha said, looking pleased. "Are we all ready, then? Let's go to the Labyrinth!"

The six girls went out to meet the rest of the campers.

Lucy and some of the other camp counsellors handed out helmets with lights fixed to the front and they all set off together through the campsite.

After a short walk, they arrived at the caves. "I'll just do a quick head count to make sure we've got everyone," Lucy said as they gathered at the entrance. She walked around, counting under her breath. "Nineteen, twenty, twenty-one…"

She frowned. "That's weird. I thought we'd only have eighteen people here. Have I counted wrong?"

She took a large red rucksack off her back and rummaged through it, pulling out a register. "I'll call out the names, then we can see who we've got," she decided. "Emily Adams?"

As Lucy went through the register, Kirsty noticed a group of campers sneaking off into the cave! "Rachel," she hissed. "Look!"

Rachel's eyes widened. "I'm sure I saw a flash of green," she whispered. "They must be goblins!"

Ashley peered over the top of Rachel's pocket to see. "Why are they going into the cave?" she wondered in her tiny silvery voice.

"Kirsty Tate?" called Lucy just then.

"Here!" Kirsty replied.

"And Rachel Walker," Lucy said.

"Here," Rachel said.

Lucy looked relieved. "OK – that's everyone," she said. "I must have been having a dippy moment when I was counting. Let's go into the Labyrinth!"

The group went into the mountainside, along a rocky tunnelled path that led out into a huge, high cavern. It was very eerie. Their voices echoed against the cave walls and they could hear water dripping in the distance. "These are limestone caves," one of the counsellors told the group, shining her torch up to the roof of the cavern. "Up there are what's called stalactites – do you see? They look rather like rock icicles."

"And if you think they're impressive, wait until we get to the maze," another counsellor added. "There are tunnels after tunnels after tunnels – and just as you're starting to feel really lost, you come out into this magnificent cave full of the most enormous stalactites you've ever seen."

Lucy, meanwhile, was unzipping her jacket. "It's warm in here," she said in surprise. "Usually it's much cooler than this. And wetter too – but the path isn't slippery at all today, is it? I'm even going to take my gloves off!"

Rachel looked down and saw that Lucy was right. The rocky ground beneath their feet looked bone dry except for… She frowned and bent lower to take a closer look. There on the ground was a set of tiny, clawed footprints – and they were shimmering with magic!

"Kirsty, Ashley," she hissed, her voice trembling with excitement. "Look – I think the baby dragon may have come this way!"

Searching for Sizzle

Ashley's face lit up with a grin. "That is definitely a dragon's trail. Sizzle must have been here!" she whispered. "And that explains why the cave is so warm: dragons give off lots of heat, especially if they have a cold and keep sneezing out flames!"

"So that's why the goblins are here, too," Kirsty worked out. "They must be looking for Sizzle. I hope they haven't found him yet."

"Can you all get into small groups, please?" Lucy called at that moment. "We're going to have a race now, and the first team to reach the centre of the Labyrinth wins. Watch out for the uneven floors, and no running! Ready, steady...go!"

The campers all headed off into the maze of tunnels. Rachel and Kirsty struck out alone with Ashley, who flew out of her hiding place to flutter alongside them. If Sizzle was somewhere in the caves, they had to find the dragon before the goblins or any of the campers got to him!

"Oh!" Rachel gasped suddenly. She stopped and pointed at the wall ahead. There they could see the shadow of a goblin's big nose and the safety helmet he wore on his head. "He must be just around the corner," she whispered, feeling her heart thud a little faster.

She, Kirsty and Ashley moved towards the shadow. But the goblin must have heard the girls' footsteps because he began running, just managing to stay out of their reach as he pelted through the tunnels.

Kirsty noticed a series of black marks along the walls as they went by. "These are strange," she said, and ran a finger along one of them. It came away black with soot.

"They must be scorch marks from Sizzle's sneezes," Ashley guessed. "We're getting closer to him!"

The girls could hear the voices of the other campers coming from the nearby tunnels. Then, as they turned around a corner, they bumped straight into a group of three goblins – and they all fell over at once.

Kirsty and Rachel scrambled to their
feet, as did the goblins. Ashley perched
on Kirsty's shoulder, looking wary.

The goblins seemed a bit jumpy about
something. "It's only silly girls," one of
them muttered, his face a paler shade
of green than normal. "Nothing scary."

Another goblin scowled. "I wasn't
scared," he blustered. "Anyway, come on,
we've got work to do. We're on a dragon
hunt! And we're going to catch it before
any of those interfering fairies!"

The Pogwurzel Plan

Rachel and Kirsty exchanged anxious glances, both thinking frantically. They had to think of a way to stop the goblins getting to Sizzle!

Luckily, a brilliant idea popped into Rachel's head and she winked at Kirsty, hoping her friend would play along with her. "Be careful, then," she said meaningfully, speaking directly to the goblin who looked particularly pale and nervous. "Because you get lots of Pogwurzels in these caves, you know."

The goblins stared. "Pogwurzels?" they echoed, their eyes dark with fear.

Rachel and Kirsty both knew that there were no such creatures as Pogwurzels – but goblin mothers often told naughty goblin children that if they didn't behave, a Pogwurzel would come and get them.

Lots of younger goblins still believed
in Pogwurzels – and were very scared
of them!

Kirsty hid a smile as she joined the
conversation. "Didn't you know?" she
asked the goblins. "Pogwurzels love caves.
They like being in dark, scary places –
especially if there are goblins to chase."

While Kirsty was talking, Rachel asked
Ashley in a whisper if she would fly
around the corner. "And when you hear
me shout the word 'Pogwurzel', make
a really scary sound!" she added.

Ashley grinned.
"Leave it to me,"
she whispered
back, and
slipped away
unnoticed.

Then Rachel pretended to gasp in surprise. "Look – what's that?" she cried in a frightened voice, pointing behind the goblins. "I think I just saw one!"

The goblins turned in fright, clutching at each other and looking very scared.

"And there's another!" Kirsty cried, pointing into a shadowy corner.

"I want my mummy," whimpered one of the goblins, staring around nervously.

"I want to go home!" cried another, his lower lip wobbling.

"There's a Pogwurzel!" Rachel yelled
in a loud voice – and right on cue,
Ashley used her magic to create a
ferocious-sounding roar!

"Help!" shrieked the goblins, scattering
from the cave. "Let's get out of here!"

Ashley fluttered back
to the girls, grinning
in delight.

"That worked
brilliantly," she
said. "Well done
– what an
imaginative
idea! Now let's
keep searching.
I can sense Sizzle
is close by, in the
centre of the maze."

"Great – what are we waiting for?" Kirsty said eagerly. "Let's get through this maze as soon as we can!"

Unfortunately, it wasn't quite as easy as that. The girls kept jogging through the tunnels but found dead end after dead end. The rocky walls looked so similar, it was difficult to get their bearings, and after a few minutes they felt completely lost.

Just as Kirsty was starting to despair, they heard a loud sneeze. "Bless you!" she said automatically and then smiled. "Hey – might that be Sizzle?" But then she frowned. Something strange seemed to be happening to her. It felt as if all her ideas and imagination were draining away. Everything seemed grey in her mind.

Rachel was also feeling peculiar. She shook her head. "Something's wrong," she said anxiously. "It's as if a light bulb has been switched off in my mind. I know we should be thinking about what to do next…but nothing's happening in my brain."

"Me too," Kirsty said, clutching the sides of her head. "Why can't we think properly? This is horrible!"

Fairy Flying

"I think I know what's happening," Ashley said. "Don't worry – it's Sizzle who's causing this. Because he's nervous, his powers are working in reverse and so your imagination is disappearing temporarily."

Almost as soon as she'd finished speaking, that all changed. Suddenly, ideas were pouring into the girls' heads, almost faster than they could think.

"Hey – I know what we could do!"
Kirsty said, beaming.

"Oh yes – I've
just had a
great idea
how we can
help Sizzle,
too," Rachel
said excitedly.

Ashley chuckled. "It looks as though
Sizzle's magical powers are working
properly again, and boosting your
imagination!" she said.

It wasn't just Kirsty and Rachel who
were full of ideas. In the tunnels all
around them they could hear other
campers talking excitedly. "I've thought
of a brilliant story about being here in
the cave," a girl in the next tunnel said.

"A song about a funny cave-monster has just popped into my head," laughed a boy in delight nearby.

"You could make up a cool ghost story set in these caves," a third person said.

"Everyone's getting closer to Sizzle and the centre of the maze," Kirsty realised. "We've got to find him quickly, before anyone else does!"

Ashley nodded. "I'll turn you into fairies," she said, waving her wand over them. "That way we can all fly together and go much quicker!"

Green fairy dust swirled around Kirsty and Rachel and they found themselves shrinking smaller and smaller, until they were the same size as Ashley. They were fairies again! Kirsty fluttered her wings and zoomed into the air. "What are we waiting for?" she cried. "Let's go!"

The three fairy friends flew at top speed through the maze. All around, they could hear pounding footsteps and excited laughter as the other campers tried to find the middle.

Luckily, the fairies could go much faster than anyone else! Within a few moments they'd reached the maze's centre – and there was a small green scaly dragon hovering in mid-air, with black puffs of smoke coming from his nostrils.

"Sizzle!" cried Ashley happily.

At the sound of her voice, his ears pricked up – and a big smile spread across his face as he saw his fairy mistress.

Sizzle raced through the air towards her, growing smaller and smaller as he did so. By the time he reached Ashley, he was tiny and able to leap into her arms for a cuddle.

"Oh, he's so cute!" cried Rachel in delight, flying over to pet him. Kirsty couldn't resist either, and Sizzle made the funniest little roaring purrs they had ever heard.

"We must be nearly there now," a voice rang out just then. "Hurry – I think it's this way!"

The fairies exchanged anxious glances.
The campers were approaching. Ashley
quickly waved her wand over Kirsty and
Rachel, and with a flood of glittery
sparkles, they were turned back into girls.

"Thank you so much," Ashley said hastily. "Now I can take Sizzle back to Fairyland and finish his training. I'd better fly!"

In a last shower of fairy dust, she was gone – just as Lucy emerged from one of the tunnels. "Kirsty, Rachel, well done!" she cried, smiling. "You're the first ones here. No one's ever made it to the centre so fast before! How did you manage to find your way so quickly?"

Other boys and girls were now
pouring into the central area from the
different tunnels around the cave – all
chatting and laughing happily.

Kirsty and Rachel shared a knowing
look. "I guess we just used our
imagination," Kirsty replied.

"It was really good fun," Rachel
added truthfully. She gave Kirsty a secret
smile as Lucy went off to talk to some

of the other campers. The holiday
was already shaping up to be very
exciting … and with six of the young
Magical Animals left to find, the girls
were sure there were plenty more
adventures to come!

Now Rachel and Kirsty
must help...

Lara the Black Cat Fairy

Read on for a sneak peek...

"Come on, Kirsty." Rachel Walker picked up her rucksack and smiled at her best friend, Kirsty Tate. "It's time for our next activity – we're going on an orienteering expedition."

"Oh, great!" Kirsty exclaimed happily, lacing up her walking boots. "I'm really looking forward to it." Then she grinned. "To be honest, I'm not exactly sure what an orienteering expedition is, though!"

Rachel and the other girls in the cabin, Emma, Natasha, Katie and Catherine, smiled warmly at Kirsty.

"Orienteering is using a compass and a map to find your way to a meeting-place," Emma explained. "All the different teams try to get there first. It's great fun."

"It sounds fantastic," Kirsty agreed.

"I've enjoyed every activity here at camp so far," Rachel remarked to Kirsty, as their room-mates went outside.

Kirsty nodded. "And it's been even *more* exciting since our fairy friends asked for our help!" she whispered.

On the day the girls arrived at the camp, they discovered that Jack Frost had been up to his old tricks in Fairyland again. This time, he and his naughty goblin servants had kidnapped seven Magical Animals from the Magical Animal Fairies.

The Magical Animals were very rare

and precious because they helped to
spread the kind of magic that every
human and fairy could possess – the
magic of imagination, luck, humour,
friendship, compassion, healing and
courage. The fairies trained the Magical
Animals for a whole year to make sure
they knew how to use their powers to
spread their wonderful gifts throughout
the human and the fairy worlds.

Read Lara the Black Cat Fairy to find out
what adventures are in store for Kirsty and Rachel!

Meet the Magical Animal Fairies

Seven magical animals are lost in the human world! Help Rachel and Kirsty reunite them with their fairy friends.

www.rainbowmagicbooks.co.uk

Meet the fairies, play games
and get sneak peeks at
the latest books!

www.rainbowmagicbooks.co.uk

There's fairy fun for everyone on
our wonderful website.
You'll find great activities, competitions, stories and
fairy profiles, and also a special newsletter.

Get 30% off all Rainbow Magic books at

www.rainbowmagicbooks.co.uk

Enter the code RAINBOW at the checkout.
Offer ends 31 December 2013.

Offer valid in United Kingdom and Republic of Ireland only.

Win Rainbow Magic Goodies!

There are lots of Rainbow Magic fairies, and we want to know which one is your favourite! Send us a picture of her and tell us in thirty words why she is your favourite and why you like Rainbow Magic books. Each month we will put the entries into a draw and select one winner to receive a Rainbow Magic Sparkly T-shirt and Goody Bag!

Send your entry on a postcard to Rainbow Magic Competition, Orchard Books, 338 Euston Road, London NW1 3BH.
Australian readers should email: childrens.books@hachette.com.au
New Zealand readers should write to Rainbow Magic Competition, 4 Whetu Place, Mairangi Bay, Auckland NZ.
Don't forget to include your name and address.
Only one entry per child.

Good luck!

Meet the Green Fairies

Rachel and Kirsty must rescue the Green Fairies'
magic wands from Jack Frost, before
the environment is damaged!

www.rainbowmagicbooks.co.uk